MW01284137

Wild
Justice

OTHER TITLES BY SANDI AULT

A **WILD** MYSTERY
SHORT STORY

Wild Justice

SANDI AULT

HandInPaw

HANDINPAW PUBLISHING

Published by HandInPaw Publishing ©2018 Sandi Ault
In the Rocky Mountains of Colorado, USA

This is a work of fiction. Names, characters, places, and incidents either are the product of the author's imagination or are used fictitiously, and any resemblance to actual persons, living or dead, business establishments, events, or locales is entirely coincidental.

Printing History:
WILD JUSTICE was originally published in ELLERY QUEEN MYSTERY MAGAZINE in 2012
The digital version was first published as an electronic/digital book in 2014 by HandInPawPublishing ©Sandi Ault

Cover copyright ©2014 Sandi Ault
   Cover layout design copyright © 2018 Sandi Ault
   Images & cover layout by Eric Schodde/ES Creative Design

All rights reserved. No part of this publication can be reproduced, scanned, distributed, or transmitted in any form or by any means, electronic, mechanical, or otherwise, without permission in writing from Sandi Ault. Contact: www.sandiault.com

THIS EDITION ©2018 by Sandi Ault all rights reserved
Published in the United States of America by HandInPaw Publishing
www.sandiault.com

ISBN-13: 978-1-7335099-2-3

PRAISE FOR THE WILD MYSTERY SERIES

"Scenes of the high, dry, glittering landscape are as clean as a sun-bleached bone, and there are thrills galore…"
— *New York Times Book Review* (WILD INDIGO)

"Ault uses her knowledge of the high, dry West to give us a look at Pueblo Indian culture."
— *Tony Hillerman* (WILD INDIGO)

"Crackles with life and novelty."
— *The Washington Post* (WILD INDIGO)

"Smashing."
— *C. J. Box* (WILD INDIGO)

"Simply put, a page-turner of the highest order."
— *The Barnes and Nobel Review* (WILD INDIGO)

"Ault has another page turner…"
— *Richmond Times Dispatch* (WILD INFERNO)

"Ault is such a good writer that crime fiction buffs who enjoy a good mystery with plenty of action and great background detail will put this on their hold lists. Highly recommended."
— *Library Journal* STARRED REVIEW (WILD INFERNO)

"The vivacious Ault knows whereof she writes in Wild Inferno…Where Ault excels is in developing a suspenseful, action-filled mystery on rugged Southwest terrain."
— *New Mexico Magazine* (WILD INFERNO)

"She's a master at describing nature."
— *Albuquerque Journal* (WILD SORROW)

"Ault's talents go far beyond devising a suspense-driven plot..."
—*New Mexico Magazine* (WILD SORROW)

"A crackling mystery, 'Wild Sorrow' also combines Ault's lovely nature writing with her indignation over the way Indian children were mistreated at the boarding schools. It's a potent mix, and Ault invests it with chilling authenticity and suspense — and an epilogue that will break your heart.
—*Richmond Times Dispatch* (WILD SORROW)

"Fans of the late Tony Hillerman will embrace Ault's outstanding third mystery... Ault's wildlife expertise and knowledge of Tanoah culture enhance a poignant plot."
—*Publishers Weekly,* STARRED REVIEW (WILD SORROW)

"Verdict: Ault's love of the outdoors and her respect for American Indian culture are evident in her vivid descriptions of the culture, people, and northern New Mexico landscape. ... Nevada Barr fans and mystery aficionados still mourning the late Tony Hillerman will snap this one up as well as other titles in the Mary Higgins Clark Award-winning series. Enthusiastically recommended."
—*Library Journal* STARRED REVIEW (WILD PENANCE)

"If you enjoy the outdoors, the mysticism of Indian cultures, along with breakneck adventure, Ault's WILD series might just get your heart racing."
—*The Charlotte Observer* (WILD PENANCE)

"...a set of mysteries that leave fans breathless by the end of the first chapter."
—*Sedona Red Rock News*

"Ault is often compared to the late Tony Hillerman. While it's an honorable and helpful comparison, it's also a bit unfair. Ault's novels are unique and original, and they deserve to stand on their own. ...Ault's WILD INFERNO was recognized by Publishers Weekly as one of the Best Books of [the year]. ...Ault, like many a great storyteller of the American West, understands the richness of 'deep time.' And we are fortunate she has once again given us a glimpse into the great heritage of a great people."
—*Estes Park Trail Gazette*

"Ault has the background to write this outdoor series, and it shows on every page. ...You might as well turn off the phone and lock the door, you are in it until the very last page releases its hold on you. About the book: The suspense is one thing — and there is plenty of it — but you will feel like you're reading a literary work at the same time. Ault uses the language in unique ways."
—*The Coloradoan*

"Ault's portrait of Pueblo life and the conflict of cultures she dramatizes are integral to her rousing debut."
—*Kirkus Reviews*

"Tinged with mysticism, this artfully told story should appeal to fans of Nevada Barr...Tony Hillerman... and Margaret Coel."
—*Publishers Weekly*

"Read this for outdoor adventure and take a walk on the Wild side."
—*Rocky Mountain News*

"This edge-of-the-seat sequel to Ault's successful debut, WILD INDIGO, demonstrates her skill at weaving together plot lines, complex characters, and lots of suspense."
—*Library Journal* BEST BOOKS OF THE YEAR LIST

"Ault smoothly blends a murder mystery plot with Native American lore in this impressive sequel..."
—*Publishers Weekly* BEST BOOKS OF THE YEAR LIST

"Fast and furious...The mystery deepens with every page."
—*The Charlotte Observer*

"The fiery descriptions of the blaze's terrifying power are worth the price of admission, but Ault also keeps the pages turning...A writer with a flair for the outdoors, Ault deserves a large following."
—*Rocky Mountain News* (WILD INFERNO)

For the wolves...

*and for all those who love
the WILD
and work to preserve and protect it*

Wild Justice

A WILD MYSTERY SHORT STORY

1: ALMOST

She was the last one, and he might have already killed her, too, if I hadn't happened along when I did. She was bleeding, in pain, her eyes wild with fear. I raised my rifle, looked through the scope and slowly panned 360, making sure no one was watching. Satisfied that we were alone, I left the rifle on the ground by my Jeep, pulled the metal detector from the back, and—out of habit—touched my hand to the holster that held my Sig Sauer on my belt, like a gambler kisses the dice before a roll that can make or break him. I turned on the detector and crept slowly forward, listening for its alert, still panning my eyes across the landscape.

I wanted to move more quickly, but the killer had been known to set multiple traps in one place, and I wasn't going to end up stepping in one if I could help it. And the last time I'd come upon one of his victims still alive, he'd shot her in the head with a high-powered rifle from some unseen location, just as I was attempting to disarm the trap.

Kewa, a new mother with babies born only three weeks before, lay helpless on the ground in front of me. One by one, all of the other pack members who normally would have provided for her and the cubs had been trapped, forcing Kewa to leave her babies to hunt. She was dreadfully thin, not a good sign. Although she had raised her head and watched me warily when I drove up and first got out of my Jeep, she now lay quietly, resigned to whatever fate awaited her. Her breathing was rapid and shallow, and a pool of blood stained the carpet of pine needles beneath her ragged back leg. Fortunately, I'd gotten to her before she'd tried to chew it off. I hadn't been so lucky with several of the other members of the now-nearly-extinct Pintado wolf pack.

Satisfied that there were no other traps around her, I set the detector on the ground, squatting down to put her more at ease. Kewa's eyes followed me, but she did not raise her head again—she was probably too weak. I started to coo softly to her. "You're going to be all right, girl. I'm going to help you. And if I can find your den, I'll help your babies, too. I'm going to touch you now, okay? I just want you to see that I'm not going to hurt you so you'll let me get you out of that trap." I reached my hand forward, palm up, and brushed the tips of my fingers against the middle of her spine. She flinched at my touch, and her head came up slightly. But when she sensed that I wasn't going to hurt her—or perhaps because she no longer had the strength to defend herself—she lowered her head once more. I continued to touch her back, first lightly, and then with more pressure, stroking to reassure her. I could feel every detail of her spine through her thick coat, no fat under the skin and precious little muscle. Still touching her with my left hand, I reached with my right and pulled the bandana from my back pocket. Holding it behind me so I wouldn't alarm her, I shook the cloth square open, then held it up by one corner so that she could see it. I fluttered it a little, but she didn't respond. That meant she was ready. I draped the cloth over her face, covering her head completely. She didn't move. Now I could get her out of the trap, put a tourniquet on that leg, and get her into the back of my car and down to the wildlife rehabilitation center for emergency care. As I lifted her body and ran with her to the Jeep, she went limp in my arms, unconscious. She didn't weigh much more than forty pounds, by my guess, but she had been tagged and weighed last summer at a healthy sixty-two. Starvation and hungry pups had taken her down to little more than skin and bones.

I raced down the rocky, rutted dirt trail, through snowmelt mud-bogs and over icy slickrock, all the way willing Kewa to hold on just a little while longer. A half-hour later, I was out of the mountains and within radio range. I thumbed the mike and alerted the dispatcher: "This is Jamaica Wild with the Bureau of Land Management. I have an injured wolf, code red. Need a triage team at the wildlife center, ETA twenty minutes from now." When I blazed into the parking lot, a trio of techs in scrubs rushed out the door with a cart and med kits. I dashed around to the back of the Jeep and opened the hatch, fervently praying that Kewa wouldn't be like all the other ones. As one medic huddled into the back and held a stethoscope to Kewa's chest, I noticed I was holding my breath.

I feared the worst, but I had to know. My voice crackled with uncontrolled emotion as I spoke, "Did she make it?"

CHAPTER 2: THE TRAP

At the BLM's Taos field offices, I entered the lobby and headed fast down the hall to the Boss's office. I walked in without knocking, threw my jacket and hat in one chair and dropped into the other, facing Roy's desk.

He glanced up from his paperwork, noticed the bloodstains on the front of my shirt and jeans, and tilted his head to one side. His eyes narrowed slightly as he looked into my face. "How many does that make now?"

"Eleven."

"Same M.O.?"

"It's him."

"Did you take the trap by the sheriff's office for fingerprints?"

"It wouldn't do any good, Boss. He always wears gloves. We've failed to get prints off of so many traps that the deputies have a poll going to see how many I get. It's starting to be a joke to them. Helping me find a trapper is pretty much rock-bottom on their priorities list."

"But we might get lucky with one of those traps. This could be the one."

"I want to get more than lucky with this guy."

"Yeah, I know, Jamaica. I do, too. We might have three or four dozen grey wolves left in the whole state of New Mexico. We got people shooting wolves, poisoning them, and this sonofabitch who likes to see them suffer when he kills them. All by himself, in just three months, he's decimated over twenty-percent of the species in the entire state."

I put my hand to my chest and began to rub in a circle. "It's worse than that. This time he trapped a nursing bitch. There's a litter of pups somewhere; I've got to find them before he does. Even if he doesn't go looking for them, I've got to find the den before those babies starve or freeze, or both."

Roy stood up and rounded the corner of the desk, perched on the edge of the front and looked at me. "How are you going to do that? Did she leave tracks?"

"No, the ground was frozen."

"You could call Charlie Dorn over at Game and Fish and see if he can help."

"I already did. He gave me some data from the radio collars they had on three other Pintado wolves before this guy got them. We're going to mark the points on a map and try to figure out where the den might be."

"Well, a pack of wolves has to roam a lot of real estate in winter to keep everybody fed. I don't know how you're going to narrow it down; you don't have much time. I wish I had someone to team with you on this, but you know how it is. Charlie didn't have anyone he could send out to help look for the den?"

"Nope," I said, standing up. "He's in the same situation as we are—skeleton crew."

Roy shook his head. "Well, hell. You be sure and use that metal detector. Don't go anywhere without it."

"I will, Boss." I picked up my hat and coat. "Gotta go, I'm losing daylight."

"Jamaica, one more thing."

I half-turned in the doorway.

"If you're not going to take that trap to the S.O. for fingerprints, put it out back in the shed. We might need it for evidence if we can ever bring this guy to trial—but in the meantime, those traps cost money, and if we keep taking them from him, he'll surely run out sooner or later. And we all know he's not rich enough to keep buying more."

I didn't look at Roy. "I didn't get the trap this time."

"What? Tell me you didn't leave it out there for someone—or something—else to step in and get hurt!"

I started fumbling with my hat and jacket. "There wasn't time. I was way back in the mountains, and the wolf was critical."

"You're a resource protection agent; you can't leave a trap out on public lands, no matter how remote the area."

I hesitated, cleared my throat. "Don't worry. When I was getting her out, I disabled it."

"But that's no good either. Now our wolf-killer can retrieve it, fix it, and get himself another lobo with it!"

"No, he can't. It won't work for him anymore."

"Well, I want it for evidence, and I want to deprive him of having it, even for parts. When you go back to look for the cubs, you get that trap and bring it in, you hear me?"

"Understood." I pushed my hat onto my head and slung the bloody jacket over one shoulder.

"You be careful out there, and radio in as soon as you're back in range," Roy called as I made my way down the hall and out the front door.

In the parking lot, I looked around before I opened the rear hatch of my Jeep. Middle of a weekday in winter, no one in sight. Not at the BLM nor at the Forest Service Offices next door. Besides my vehicle, I saw just a few cars belonging to the administrative personnel who worked year-round. I unlocked the rear compartment, lifted the hatch, and threw my jacket in the cargo area. I grabbed a hoodie out of my pack, straightened, and quickly pulled it over my head, thrust one arm into it and then the other while I continued to scan my surroundings. Then I reached in and spread the jacket out flat so that it completely covered the trap.

CHAPTER 3: LIKE A WOLF

Based on experience, I was pretty sure that Casta Diaz hadn't seen me rescue Kewa. Two times before, when I'd gotten to a wolf before it died or chewed off its leg, he'd shot out my tires so I couldn't get to the wildlife center in time to save the animal. Last week, he'd fired a round into the skull of a yearling female just as I was freeing her from the trap. And this was precisely why I knew for certain that Diaz was the killer.

Casta Diaz had two outstanding attributes: he was an expert marksman with long-range weapons, and he had a chip on his shoulder as big as a truck. He'd come by the first of these honestly: while in the army, he'd trained as a sniper in the elite special forces school at Fort Benning. But it turned out that, in spite of being a phenomenal distance shooter, Diaz wasn't good military material. He'd failed to qualify for a tactical assignment due to repeated altercations with his fellow soldiers. Instead, he was transferred to a supply unit which soon shipped out for Iraq. A local army reserves sergeant who had been deployed there at the same time told me that Diaz was known for shooting dogs in Baghdad as well as taking odds on how many golden jackals he could kill when they came out to forage at night near the green zone. "He cut off a paw from every one of those dogs," the sergeant said, "and he had over two hundred of them hanging on a wire outside his quarters before they finally made him take them down."

But it wasn't until his second tour of duty overseas, this time in Afghanistan, that Diaz's military career came to an end. Casta was a person of interest in the rape and torture of a local woman who was burned to death, and during questioning, he assaulted an officer. When the army couldn't produce enough evidence to charge Diaz for the death of the Afghani woman, they gave him a dishonorable discharge for the latter offense.

Since his return stateside, every law enforcement officer in northern New Mexico had reason to like Diaz for an unsolved case. He was a suspect in a plethora of crimes, from dog poisoning and arson to a drive-by shooting. But the evidence always proved too insubstantial to convict. Casta was arraigned twice for beating his girlfriend, who ultimately dropped the charges in these incidents but then mysteriously disappeared after filing a third complaint of assault and battery. After his father obtained a restraining order against him, Diaz moved out of the family home and took up living on public lands, in remote areas where he was unlikely to be charged with squatting. He moved his camp frequently during the summer and autumn, then began holing up in caves once winter set in. The rest of the law moved on to other cases, relieved that Casta Diaz was my problem now.

If luck was on my side, Diaz didn't know about the den with the pups, since he hadn't gotten to Kewa after she'd had the misfortune to step in his trap. He might not have had a chance to discover—and possibly didn't know beforehand, as I did from working with Charlie Dorn at Game and Fish—that she was a nursing mother. Just the same, I knew Diaz would be out there. If I found the den, there was a good chance that he would find it, too, because he would be watching me.

I stopped for gas and provisions before I left Taos, and while the tank was filling, I spread a topographical map over the hood of the Jeep and called Dorn. "I mapped the GPS data you sent me from the three Pintado wolves' radio collar tags, but they roamed a vast area. There's no way I can cover it all in time."

"I know," Dorn said. "Let's try this: never mind the other wolves, where'd you find Kewa?"

I traced my finger along the terrain, then read him the lat and long.

"Okay, I'm looking at my map. The den will be somewhere close by. A mama wolf wouldn't have gone too far away from her babies if she could find mice or other small rodents to feed upon. And she would have placed her den someplace fairly near to water."

I used a pen to mark the place where I'd found Kewa, then opened my pocket knife and measured the length of the blade against the scale in the map's legend. I set the point of the pen against a serration on the blade, pressed the tip of the knife on the spot I'd just marked, and used this as a compass to draw a circle on the map representing two miles in every direction from that central point. I studied the topography inside the sphere. "There's a small, seasonal mountain stream that winds through an area just over a half-mile to the west of where I found her."

"I see it," Charlie said, "but it's probably dry right now. Won't fill until the snowpack starts to melt in late spring."

"It's the only water source in a two-mile radius. The den has to be somewhere near there."

"You might be right. I know this doesn't narrow it down much, but let me tell you what you're looking for. You want to find a berm or a small cave that's south-or-east-facing. It will be on fairly high ground, with a ledge or some high meadow right above it or nearby—something that would make a good vantage point and would accommodate the other members of the pack."

"That could be anyplace," I said, shaking my head.
"I know. You're going to have to think like a wolf."

CHAPTER 4: KILL ZONE

The Pintado Pack had made their home in a narrow mountain gap with sloping granite-and-earth walls forested mainly with ponderosa pines. I couldn't afford to have Diaz target my tires again once I found the cubs, so I left my Jeep behind a rock outcropping at the top of the lowest peak overlooking the valley, the one bordering it on the east. At 6,300 feet, it still meant quite a hike in—and I would have to rely on my strength and agility to get out quickly on foot. I suspected the den was on the opposite side, on the east-facing slope, but there were no trails on that side for me to drive in closer.

Instead of my orange high-tech pack, I had brought an old brown canvas one that weighed more but would blend in better with the terrain. I packed the bare essentials I needed to survive and to bring the wolf cubs out: the metal detector, my rifle, handgun, and knife; binoculars; a dozen slap-activated hand-warmers, a deerskin and a foil space blanket for the wolf cubs; a flashlight and headlamp; and as little water as I could make do with because of its added weight to my pack. No food—I knew that if I hadn't found the den by morning, the pups wouldn't make it. Without milk and warmth from their mother, they would be lucky to survive the night. I took out the tin of brown shoe polish I'd purchased in town and rubbed it on my face and over the backs of my hands. I still wore the same bloodstained jeans and boots, but now I added a camouflage jacket over my hoodie and tucked my long, blonde hair up into a stocking cap. I wound black electrical tape over the yellow handle on the metal detector and rubbed shoe polish over its aluminum shaft so I wouldn't reveal myself with a flash of reflected glint or bright color as I moved through the valley. My radio was useless in this terrain—too many peaks and canyons for the line-of-sight necessary to transmit and receive, so I left it in the Jeep.

I started moving down the slope through the trees, avoiding exposure, even though it cost me time to weave in and out of cover. I held the metal detector out before me with my left hand and kept my rifle slung on a strap over my shoulder, leaving one hand free to stabilize myself as I descended through the trees and over rock ledges. It was a steep slope, and my boots slipped and slid and crunched against roots and brush, creating little landslides of stones and twigs that seemed to amplify a thousand-fold in the silence of the wild. If another wolf were present in this valley, she would know that I was there, moving into her territory. The question was: *did Diaz know?*

I pushed downward toward the seasonal stream I'd pinpointed on the map; it was less than a mile from where I'd found Kewa. I hoped I'd guessed right in thinking that this little water course might be blessed with enough snow and sunlight to hold some water in a few low places—even in the dead of winter—and that the den would be on the opposite slope above it, facing the warmth of the sun.

I stopped roughly halfway down the mountain. Crawling cautiously out of the tree cover, I stretched out flat on a round of elephant-back rock. I pushed forward to the edge, where I propped myself up on my elbows, scoping the terrain below me with my field glasses, looking for the stream channel. I couldn't make it out, but I knew I was on the right track. A tiny brook like the one I was looking for winds and weaves through narrow depressions and nourishes vegetation which can obscure it from view. I moved my binoculars up and panned the opposite slope. Directly to the west of me, a gnarled sculpture of moss rock created a similar overlook to the one I was perched upon. I focused on the area below this, looking for any sign of a den, but the tree growth was too dense. Moving my sights to the left, I looked for a more southerly overlook like the one I'd just seen. Higher up, a sloping patch of ground showed white through the trees—a small clearing covered with snow. This, too, could have been a lookout used by a wolf pack. I sighted the binoculars on the area below it, looking for tracks in the snow, trails, anything. The terrain was too heavily forested. I was going to have to pick one of these two locations, pray I'd chosen the right one, and search the area by going over it in a grid-pattern on foot. That ground would be in deep shadow by the time I got there, given that a winter dusk began early in a valley where high peaks to the west obscured the late afternoon sun. I figured I had less than an hour of daylight, and perhaps an hour more of semidark before full-on night. After that, I would either have to search by what little starlight made its way through the narrow notch of sky above or risk exposing myself by using a light.

I put the field glasses down and closed my eyes, drawing in a breath and willing my mind to quiet, breathing out the urgency, the fear; inhaling the cold, sharp, pine-scented air, the loamy smell of lichen, moss, sun-warmed ancient rock. *Grandmother Earth,* I silently prayed, *let me be a wolf today so I can find Kewa's babies.*

As I pushed back from my exposed position on the rock, I was betrayed by a raven, who cried an alarm at my movement and set up a cacophony of cawing and scolding from its fellows. This would surely give away my location if Diaz knew anything about nature. But instead of letting this concern me, when I stood once again in the cover of the trees, I saluted my ancient hunting partner, the raven. I knew its call was a sign from the Great Spirit that I was already moving out of my logical mind and into my wild wolf's brain.

As I approached the east bank of the stream bed, the metal detector set up a racket of beeping. I froze for a moment, unable to process this new and unfamiliar voice in the forest. I'd been carrying the thing for so long, listening to its low, sputtering hum, that it startled me when it went into high alert and forced me out of my wolf guise. I knew I'd found another trap; I'd set the detector to its least sensitive setting so that it wouldn't go off every time there was a pocket of ferrous material in the rocks or a small metal object on the ground. I had been headed straight for the trap, which was obscured by some fresh-cut pine branches. I carefully picked up one of the limbs, exposing the trap, then used the end of it to trigger its death-bite. The steel jaws snapped together with a deafening *whang*, the trap leapt into the air with an explosion of force, and I jumped backward and stumbled, almost falling to the ground. I drew in a sharp breath and let it out with a blast. Then I stooped to the ground and set to work. This was trap number twelve. I'd found eleven of them with wolves in their jaws. Number twelve was not going to be like the others. "No wolf for you," I said, as I stood up and carefully studied my surroundings. I drew a spiral in the air with my left hand—a sign of blessing I had learned from the local Tiwa Indians. And I called my inner wolf back to the fore. I looked up into the trees and spotted one of my raven companions. "Guide me," I said, and he immediately took flight to the west. I moved off in the same direction.

But the raven did not know. Or if he did, he couldn't tell me that I was walking right into another trap.

CHAPTER 5: HUNG

When the noose snapped around my ankles, I took flight. My feet catapulted up into the air, high above my head and into the trees, capsizing me and yanking my body into a high-speed inversion as a hailstorm of my gear plummeted downward. I dropped the metal detector and groped for my rifle, which eluded me, the strap sliding off my shoulder as it fell toward the ground. The field glasses went, too, striking me hard in the chin as the strap slipped off my neck. All the while a bell clanged loudly from somewhere below me. I swung back and forth, my right ankle burning painfully where the rope strangled it right through my boot. I twisted my upper body to one side and looked up. My left boot crossed atop my right foot but the lower ankle had taken most of the snap of the noose. Now my full body weight tightened the rope's grip and compressed both ankles together in a chokehold. I felt blood rushing to my head as I hung upside down, and I also felt a trickle of blood wind down my jawbone, past my left eye at the temple, and into my hair inside the stocking cap—this from where the field glasses had struck me in the chin on their way down. The bell stopped clanging as my swinging slowed; I was no longer triggering the striker, which worked like a pendulum with my body as a counterweight.

Before I could think what to do, I heard crashing in the brush as someone rushed downslope from above and to the northwest. The sound grew closer, and then Casta Diaz came into view, his rifle aimed at my head. Thin, grizzly-bearded, with long, thick locks of black hair shooting out at all angles from beneath his ball cap, he looked like a wild man, and much older than this thirty-or-so years. A jawbite pattern of deep purple pits, rumored to have been from a dog attack when he was a child, disfigured one side of his face, making him look all the more menacing. "Well, what do we have here?"

"Lower me down!" I demanded.

"Now that sounds like a girl's voice! But you don't look so pretty with all that stuff on your face. Take off that hat, lemme see your hair." He pointed the rifle at my hat and thrust the barrel forward.

I reached with one hand and pulled off the stocking cap. My hair billowed downward into the air.

"Well," Casta said, grinning, "hello, Agent Wild. What are you doing here?"

"Lower me down!" I said again.

"You can probably get your own self down. You got a knife, don't you? What kind of a resource protection agent would you be if you didn't carry a knife in the back country?"

"It's almost twenty feet to the ground," I said, "and I'd be dropping head-first. I could break my neck. Lower me down, Diaz."

He held his rifle steady in one hand and reached with the other to rub his chin, as if he were contemplating what to do. "This could be fun," he said. "I like a little sport." He walked over to my rifle and picked it up. A foul smell wafted upward. He surely hadn't bathed in months. He spotted the metal detector and field glasses and grabbed them, too. Then he looked at me and winked. "You got a little something right there," he said, holding his rifle upright and pointing a finger to the side of his face—indicating where the trickle of blood still ran from my chin into my hair. And then he walked back into the woods, the same way he had come.

Each time I struggled to reach for the rope, it jerked the noose and squeezed my feet tighter together, wrenching the heel of my left boot harder into my tortured right ankle. I gasped with the pain, wincing as I attempted to double my body over from an inverted position so that my hands could reach the rope. To make it worse, the bell clanged every time I made an attempt, thereby notifying Diaz that I was trying to escape. After my third failure to reach the rope with my hands, I realized that I wasn't going to be able to do this quietly anyway, and I could use some momentum to help me. And so I started bending forward at the waist, then arching backward, and soon I had a rhythm going, and gradually I went from swaying slightly to swinging in a wide arc, back and forth. With each swing, I hinged from the hips and swung my torso higher and higher until, at the top of one high arc, I thrust my upper body forward into an upside down pike, grasping the rope with both hands above my boots, my knees bent just enough to allow me to hold myself in this position. I held onto the rope firmly with my left hand and carefully extracted my knife from the sheath on my belt, making sure not to let it fall as it came out. I pushed the blade against the rope just under where I gripped it, and began to saw. As I severed one strand after another, I felt the rope begin to give. And then, suddenly, my feet were free and they dropped, causing me to swing wildly. And the bell—which had sounded rhythmically in response to my swinging movements—now erupted in a rapid staccato. I knew as soon as the clanging stopped altogether that Diaz would come back for me. My left hand was cramping and my shoulder felt like it was coming apart. I couldn't hold myself by one hand for much longer, but I took a moment to steady myself. *Drop and roll,* I told myself. And that's what I did.

CHAPTER 6: HEAT SIGNATURE

The odds against finding the den were bad before; now they were a hundred times worse. Thanks to my stepping into that noose trap, Diaz knew I was here, and planned to make this a hunting game, with me as prey. And my ankle was strained or sprained, leaving me lame and in pain. I no longer had my rifle, and perhaps more importantly, the metal detector. I hoped that a dozen traps was all Diaz had. I touched my Sig Sauer, thankful that the holster's clip had held on my belt and the quick-release had kept the gun in the holster. On the other side of my belt, the flashlight remained in its case, too, which might be a small blessing, because another thing I had lost was the daylight. I limped into the thicket, hoping to gain ground before Casta got back. My ankle was swelling inside my boot; the foot felt numb and I could hardly put my weight on it. After I got some cover inside the trees, I picked up a branch to use as a walking stick, but I didn't slow for more than a few seconds. I forced myself to move upward and to the south, as quietly and quickly as I could, to the area below the open knoll I'd seen through my field glasses. If my prayers had been answered, I might find the den there.

But Diaz was not far behind me. "Wild," he called from the valley floor to the north. His voice echoed off a rock ledge above me. "You got yourself down, huh? It had to hurt to fall that far. How you doing?"

I dropped down to cross a ravine, then began to climb steadily upward, my right foot so swollen that it wouldn't flex, my hand and the walking stick taking most of the weight on that side. I must have gone at least a half-mile straight up the side of the mountain. I had to be close to the pack's overlook, and that meant I had to be close to the den.

"You find the nest yet, Wild?" Diaz's voice called, this time from directly to the north. He'd been climbing, too. He had to be using night vision or a thermal imaging device to follow me. "That's why you're here, isn't it? There's some little ones I didn't get yet, right? Well this is my valley! And I don't share it with devil dogs! So, soon as you find them, I'll know it, and I'm gonna kill those little vermin. And after that, I got something special planned for you, too."

As Diaz called out, I tried to get a fix on his location and judge the distance between us. If he was tracking me with night vision, he was less than two hundred yards away. Night vision required fragments of light and could only enhance images from a limited range on a moonless night in a dark valley like this. But if he was using thermal imaging, he could be farther away and still be able to see me because of my body heat—especially because the temperature had been dropping rapidly over the last hour and it was now well below freezing, creating better contrast. I ducked behind a large boulder, shrugged out of my pack and opened it. I took out the foil space blanket, unfolded it, and draped it like a cape over my head and shoulders and tied two corners under my chin. If Diaz was using infrared tracking, this would make it harder for him to see me. I headed upslope again, forcing my right leg in spite of the pain, keeping my head down and my arms inside the cover of the blanket as best I could.

About ten minutes later, Diaz let me know that my theory had been correct. "Wild," he called, this time from below me and a bit farther away. "Where'd you go? Did you crawl in a hole or something? You won't get out of here without me finding you. You know that, right?"

When I hadn't heard him call out for more than an hour, I knew Diaz had lost track of me. But I doubted that he'd given up. He was out there waiting, like he had waited for the jackals to come out in Baghdad, patiently anticipating his next kill-shot. I limped upslope and down in the frozen darkness in my foil cape across an imagined grid, my intuition and instincts my only guide as I tried to cover the ground where I believed the den might be. My lips were numb with cold, I'd run into branches so many times that my face was scratched and stinging, and a welt had formed on my forehead. And my right leg had started to swell like a mushroom above my boot. The pain that had once emanated from my ankle now encompassed the whole of my lower leg, and every step was agonizing. I couldn't go on. When I saw a fallen ponderosa stretched across the forest floor, I limped over to the root end of the trunk to sit down and rest. I had just settled when I heard a tiny, high-pitched whimper. I roused to full alert, my senses sharp again. I stilled my breath, my heart pounding. There it was again! Just the smallest cry, and then another voice whining in tandem.

I dropped to my hands and knees and found an opening—a space between the ground and the underside of the downed tree leading back beneath the thick roots and into the earth. I grabbed my flashlight and thrust my arm into the hole, then turned on the light. A chorus of whimpers began in earnest, but I could not see the pups. I sat up, took off my pack, pulled out the LED headlamp, and strapped it around my forehead, the tender bump smarting as the band pressed against it. I pushed my head into the den, switched on the headlamp, and began working my way in by pulling myself with my arms and pushing off the ground behind me with the toe of my left boot. The entry to the den went down and to the left and I had almost pushed the full length of my body into the tunnel when my light illuminated a knot of four trembling balls of fur nesting in a pile of dried leaves and hair.

It took me a while to make all the preparations. I used the tube of my CamelBak to give the pups water, holding them against my chest to warm them as I did. Then I prepared their travel accommodations. I activated two of the hand-warmers and lined the bottom of my pack with them, then tied the four little babes hobo-style into the deerskin and put it in my pack while I got everything else ready. Weak, hungry, and cold, the warmth instantly lulled them to sleep. Before I could put on the pack and tie the foil cape around me again, I was startled by Diaz's voice.

"Wild, I see you," he yelled. "You slipped up. I see you, and— oh, my, what's that on the ground beside you? Could that be a little devil dog? Maybe more than one?" He was close from the sound of it—not much more than a hundred yards downslope and to my left. He didn't have eyes on me yet, but he was reading my thermal image.

"Okay, Casta," I called back. "You got me. I give up." As I was speaking, I pulled on the pack, then spread the foil blanket over my head and shoulders again and tied the corners under my chin.

"Whatever that is you're putting over you, it's not enough, I can still see you," Diaz called. He was closer to my elevation, still to my left, perhaps fifty yards away now.

"I'll let you have the wolf pups," I said. "You let me go and you can have them."

There was no response.

I took all the remaining hand-warmers, turned my back as I activated them, and piled them together on the log above the opening to the den. "Do we have a deal, Diaz?" I hobbled behind the nearest big pine, then crouched and started scooting downslope to the south, keeping my body low.

I heard the first shell explode against the downed tree, the crack of the rifle's report just a split second behind it, then another, and another. "You're next, Wild," he yelled. As I had hoped, Diaz had targeted the heat signature of the hand-warmers. But my survival and that of the little wolves depended on what he would do next. Would he check to make sure he'd eliminated his last target, or would he come after me?

I had made it almost a hundred yards below the den when I heard the unmistakable snap of the two double-torsion coil-springs on the trap. Diaz let out a high-decibel scream that rang out across the valley, then followed it with a string of bellowing wails. He fired three shots with his rifle, wild shots that went to the right and left of me by fifty feet or more. Perhaps he had seen my heat signature. Or maybe he was just firing blind, desperately hoping for a hit.

I didn't stop moving, fueled now with hope and adrenalin, and I hobbled across the streambed before Diaz quit hollering, then started to make my way up the eastern peak and toward my Jeep. The weight I now carried in my pack was nothing compared to that of the cast-iron and steel trap I had hefted in. I had lied to Roy about not getting the trap, but I hadn't lied about disabling it. I had removed the release mechanism, so that—once sprung—there was no device to re-open the jaws. Casta Diaz could not open that trap on his own, not without the help of a machinist or some power tools. And I was pretty sure he couldn't get to either in time. It was too late to benefit the wolves, but I figured the mountain lions and coyotes had it rough finding enough food to feed their young in the winter.

But if Diaz did somehow survive, it would be a miracle. And I had to respect miracles, I was part of one right now.

/\/\/\/\/\

A NOTE TO MY READERS

I celebrate my love for the WILD West in this series. I love to write, to explore, to adventure, to research, and to discover. I spend all my free time hiking mountains, deserts, and canyons, searching out new sources of wonder and amazement, new places of magic and enchantment to write about. I have traveled all over the globe, but I am most at home right here in the West—in the wild places, on the rivers, the cliff ledges and high mesas, in the ruins of the ancient ones, among the art panels left by the long-ago natives of this land. I love to visit my friends and adopted family at the pueblos. And I am hurrying to write about the west and the wild places as fast as I can, because these are vanishing, as are the cultural riches of my native family, who are slowly and not-so-subtly being modernized by the world that presses in around them.

So, my WILD Mystery Series is a love song to the WILD and to the West and to all the beings of all kinds who inhabit it now but may not for long . . . or may (if we are lucky) inhabit it forever.

I am lucky enough to share my life and my journeys with loving companions: a husband, a wolf, and a wildcat.

If you enjoyed this book, I hope you will tell your friends and family, and that you will look for my other works in publication.

I invite you to visit me in my online home at:

WWW.SANDIAULT.COM

Made in the USA
Middletown, DE
28 October 2023

41383777R00026